# GO BIG BLUE!
## THE MICHIGAN WOLVERINES STORY
### NEAL BERNARDS

CREATIVE EDUCATION

Published by Creative Education
123 South Broad Street, Mankato, Minnesota 56001
Creative Education is an imprint of The Creative Company

Designed by Stephanie Blumenthal
Production design by The Design Lab
Editorial assistance by John Nichols

Photos by: Allsport USA, AP/Wide World Photos, SportsChrome,
University of Michigan, and UPI/Corbis-Bettmann

Copyright © 2000 Creative Education.
International copyrights reserved in all countries.
No part of this book may be reproduced in any form
without written permission from the publisher.
Printed in the United States of America.

**Library of Congress Cataloging-in-Publication Data**

Bernards, Neal, 1963–
Go big blue! the Michigan Wolverines story / by Neal Bernards.
p. cm. — (College football today)
Summary: Examines the history of the University of Michigan football program.
ISBN: 0-88682-979-8

1. University of Michigan—Football—History—Juvenile literature. 2. Michigan Wolverines
(Football team)—History—Juvenile literature. [1. Michigan Wolverines (Football team)—History.
2. Football—History.] I. Title. II. Series: College football today (Mankato, Minn.)

GV958.U52863B47                                                                                                1999
796.332'63'0977435—dc21                                                                              98-30934

First Edition

2 4 6 8 9 7 5 3 1

"**H**ail! to the victors valiant, Hail! to the conqu'ring heroes, Hail! Hail! to Michigan, the champions of the West!" On brilliant fall afternoons in Ann Arbor, Michigan, the words of the famous fight song thunder across the "Big House" that is Michigan Stadium. Powered by the voices of a crowd 102,501 strong, the sound is deafening, intimidating, and awe-inspiring. This is gameday at the University of Michigan, and for nearly 120 years, the Wolverines have dominated gamedays like no other school in the history of college football. With nearly 800 victories, 11 national championships, and 30 bowl-game appearances, Michigan football has set a standard of excellence that other schools can only dream of achieving.

MICHIGAN STADIUM HAS

HOUSED WOLVERINES

FOOTBALL SINCE 1927.

MICHIGAN FANS PROUDLY WEAR THEIR MAIZE AND BLUE ON THE ANN ARBOR CAMPUS (BELOW).

## A SCHOOL AND STATE

Before there was the state of Michigan, there was the University of Michigan. Founded in 1817, the university is 20 years older than its state. With its long history, the university has many stories to tell—stories of eager students, proud parents, supportive fans, strong-willed coaches, and exceptional athletes. These stories include the football greats who made Michigan gridiron history: coaches with such names as Fielding Yost, Herbert "Fritz" Crisler, Glenn "Bo" Schembechler, and dazzling players such as Bennie Oosterbaan, Tom Harmon, and Charles Woodson.

The University of Michigan's home town is Ann Arbor, a small city of 110,000 people. With a student population of more than 36,000, the university makes up a third of Ann Arbor's population and is the city's main employer. Situated just 41 miles west of Detroit, the University of Michigan plays a large role in Ann Arbor residents' athletic and social lives.

The University of Michigan started as an agricultural college, but it is known today for its excellent law school and as having one of the best four-year degree programs in the country. Michigan became a charter member of the Big Ten Conference in 1896 and has grown into a large, prestigious university with a tradition-rich sports program.

The centerpiece of Michigan athletics is its football program. At every home game, a sea of maize and blue-clad Michigan football fans fill every one of the 102,501 seats in Michigan Stadium. In fact, since 1975, Michigan has had 100,000 or more fans in attendance for 142 straight games in Ann Arbor. Since 1898, Michigan has also produced 108 All-American football players and won more games than any other major college football team.

## CHAMPIONS OF THE WEST

The Michigan Wolverines are named after a compact, tenacious animal known for never backing down from a fight, no matter what the odds. Although the wolverine's strength and fearlessness make it a perfect university mascot, there is one problem: no wolverines live in Michigan. They never have. Fielding Yost, Michigan's head football coach from 1901 to 1926, had an explanation for this mystery.

COACH FIELDING YOST (ABOVE); FRITZ CRISLER BECAME MICHIGAN'S COACH IN 1938 (BELOW).

According to Yost, wolverine pelts were traded by trappers at Sault Ste. Marie on Lake Superior. Since the fur changed hands at this Michigan port city, the pelts became known as "Michigan wolverines." Yost so enjoyed his school's nickname that he brought live wolverines into Michigan stadium in 1927, a practice he soon stopped. The legendary coach concluded, "It was obvious that the Michigan mascots had designs on the Michigan men toting them, and those designs were by no means friendly."

Wolverines football started in 1879 with a game against Racine College, but it was not until 1891 that the team had a coach and began

playing a regular schedule. Football was a very different game at the turn of the century. For example, in the first-ever Rose Bowl game in 1902, the field was 110 yards long, touchdowns and field goals counted five points apiece, forward passes were not allowed, and the game was played in two 35-minute halves—not four quarters.

Although the game was different, the results from that era were much the same as those of today; more often than not, Michigan emerged victorious. In fact, by the time the Wolverines played in that first Rose Bowl, the school had already established itself as one of the nation's most powerful programs. From 1895 through 1900, Michigan went 48–7–2 and captured the 1898 Big Ten Conference title. But even those gaudy numbers paled in comparison to the accomplishments of Fielding Yost's first team in 1901. Led by speedy halfback Willie Heston and hard-hitting fullback Neil Snow, the Wolverines capped an 11–0 season with a 49–0 thrashing of Stanford in the Rose Bowl. "We wanted to leave no doubt that we were the best team in the land," said Snow. "I think we got our point across."

What made the unblemished season even more impressive is the fact that Michigan shut out not only Stanford but also each of its other 10 opponents. Michigan outscored the opposition by an astounding 550–0 margin that season, a brutish show of force that earned the maize and blue the school's first-ever national football championship.

"OLD 98," TOM HARMON (ABOVE); STANDOUT QUARTERBACK BENNY FRIEDMAN (BELOW)

1991 HEISMAN TROPHY WINNER DESMOND HOWARD

That first title would only whet the Wolverines' appetite for more. Over the next three years, Yost's teams continued to roll, posting a combined 32–0–1 mark and capturing the national championship each season. The mighty Michigan defense surrendered a paltry 40 points over the course of the four championship seasons. "That was one tough bunch of characters," commented Yost. "They played like their lives depended on it."

During Yost's 25 seasons as head coach, Michigan went 165–29–10, won 10 Big Ten titles, and produced 20 All-Americans. Yost also served as the university's athletic director until 1941 and was instrumental in laying the foundation of Michigan's renowned athletic department. "Fielding Yost did more for the University of Michigan than anyone I know," said Bennie Oosterbaan, an All-American end for Yost and a future Wolverines head coach. "When he started here, the football team played in front of 600 people, and when he left, we played in front of 90,000. He was a real pioneer."

THE 1990 ROSE BOWL GAME (ABOVE); TAILBACK TIM BIAKABUTUKA (BELOW)

## CRISLER'S WINGS AND "OLD 98"

Following Yost's retirement, the Wolverines machine did not miss a beat. From the late 1920s through the early '30s, Big Blue rolled to two more national championships under head coach Harry Kipke.

But as America slid into the depths of the Great Depression, so did the fortunes of Michigan football. After Kipke's last four teams went a combined 10–22, a new coach was summoned to lead the program. Herbert "Fritz"

# PLAYER PORTRAIT

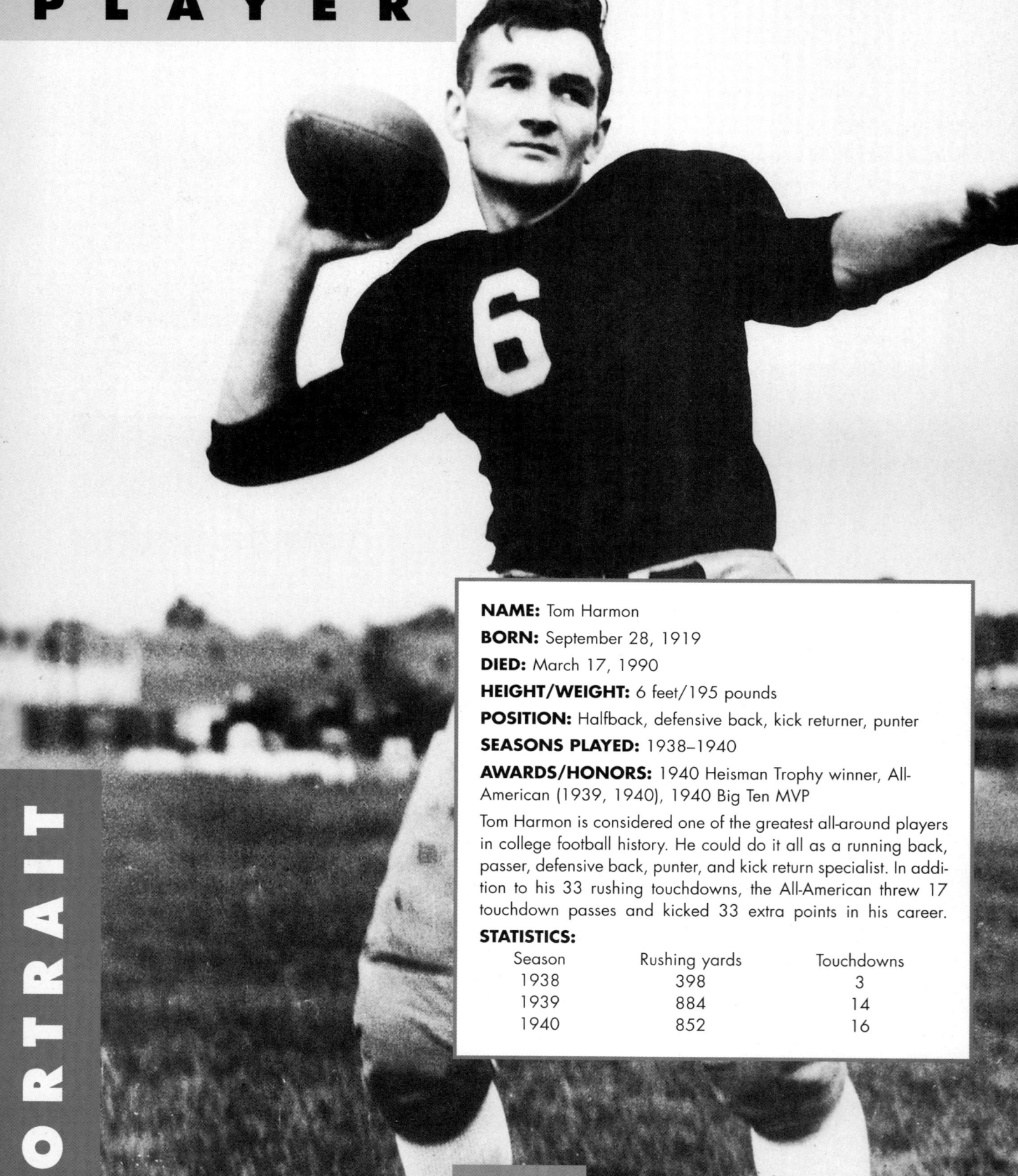

**NAME:** Tom Harmon
**BORN:** September 28, 1919
**DIED:** March 17, 1990
**HEIGHT/WEIGHT:** 6 feet/195 pounds
**POSITION:** Halfback, defensive back, kick returner, punter
**SEASONS PLAYED:** 1938–1940
**AWARDS/HONORS:** 1940 Heisman Trophy winner, All-American (1939, 1940), 1940 Big Ten MVP

Tom Harmon is considered one of the greatest all-around players in college football history. He could do it all as a running back, passer, defensive back, punter, and kick return specialist. In addition to his 33 rushing touchdowns, the All-American threw 17 touchdown passes and kicked 33 extra points in his career.

**STATISTICS:**

| Season | Rushing yards | Touchdowns |
|--------|---------------|------------|
| 1938   | 398           | 3          |
| 1939   | 884           | 14         |
| 1940   | 852           | 16         |

# COACH PORTRAIT

**NAME:** Glenn "Bo" Schembechler
**BORN:** April 1, 1929
**POSITION:** Head Coach
**SEASONS COACHED:** 1969–1989
**AWARDS/HONORS:** 13 Big Ten championships, 17 bowl game appearances
**RECORD:** 194–48–5

Bo Schembechler is the winningest coach in Michigan football history. During his 20-year reign, the stern disciplinarian led the Wolverines to 194 victories, 10 Rose Bowl appearances, and 17 finishes among the nation's top 10 teams. Schembechler's teams never endured a single losing season. His offenses were seldom flashy, but they were always rugged and disciplined. Upon retirement from coaching, he became Michigan's athletic director. Michigan honored their long-term coach by building Schembechler Hall, a football training center, locker room, and sports museum. The coaching great was also enshrined in the National Football Foundation Hall of Fame.

BO SCHEMBECHLER (ABOVE) COACHED HIS FINAL GAME IN THE 1990 ROSE BOWL (BELOW).

Crisler took the reins before the 1938 season and immediately put his personal stamp on Michigan football.

Up until 1938, Wolverines players wore plain black helmets. Coach Crisler—fresh from Princeton College, where his players wore customized helmets—decided to dress up his new team's appearance with a winged helmet design. He thought that the unique design might also help his passers see their receivers better. He apparently was right. In their first year with the new helmets, Michigan receivers doubled their reception yardage, and Wolverines passers cut their interceptions in half. Crisler's winged design has continued to strike fear in the hearts of opponents for more than 60 years.

Another major factor in the revival of Michigan's offense in 1938 was the debut of Tom Harmon, one of the most exciting players in the history of college football. Harmon, a halfback on offense and safety on defense, was known as "Old 98" for the number blazed across his chest. He twice led the nation in scoring and guided Michigan to top 20 rankings in each of his three years in uniform. His ability to leave defenders grasping at air was famous nationwide.

1997 ROSE BOWL MVP, BRIAN GRIESE

ALL-AMERICAN TACKLE

ALVIN WISTERT (ABOVE);

A 1939 GAME (BELOW)

In one game against the University of California Bears in 1940, Harmon scored two touchdowns in the first quarter. Carrying the ball on an end sweep from Michigan's 14-yard line, Harmon took off downfield for what looked like another sure touchdown. A drunken Cal spectator, however, had other ideas. Enraged by Harmon's romp over his beloved Bears, California fan Bud Brennan ran out on the field and dove at Harmon's legs. Harmon high-stepped over the would-be tackler to finish his 86-yard touchdown run. Police ejected Brennan from the stadium after his missed tackle.

Harmon later joked about the incident. "It was most embarrassing," the All-American said. "Think how I would have felt after slipping past 11 well-conditioned athletes to be downed by a woozy alum."

Harmon truly showcased his pure athletic ability in his last collegiate game, which matched the Wolverines against the Ohio State Buckeyes in Columbus, Ohio, on November 23, 1940. On that day, Harmon rushed for 139 yards, completed 11 of 12 passes for 151 yards, scored two touchdowns, kicked four extra points, intercepted three passes (running one back for a touchdown), and punted for an average of 50 yards.

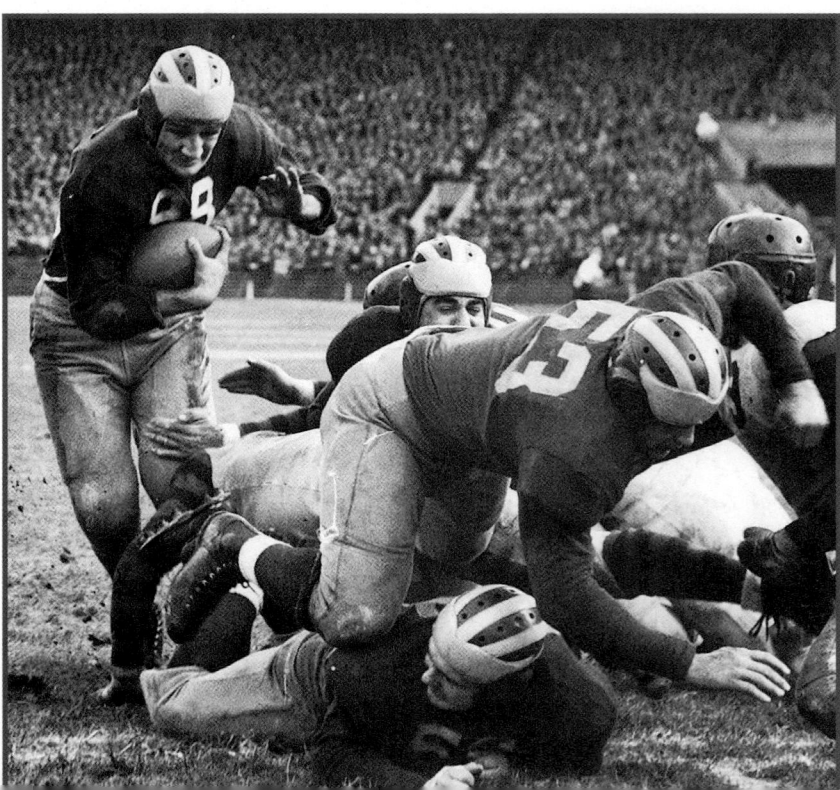

Led by Harmon's heroics, the Wolverines stomped their Big Ten rival 40–0. Harmon's game was so completely dominating that the 73,000 Ohio State fans in Columbus gave him a standing ovation when he left the game. It was a rare tribute for fans to honor the accomplishments of an opposing team's player, especially when that player hailed from Michigan.

## THE GREAT DEBATE

Before the "Bowl Championship Series" crowned a national champion, coaches and newspaper sportswriters voted in polls to determine the nation's best college football team at the end of each season. Although the system generally worked well, it could also lead to controversy. The 1947 season was one such time.

Both Notre Dame, coached by the legendary Frank Leahy, and Michigan, headed by Fritz Crisler, cruised through their regular

COACH FRITZ CRISLER

AND TACKLE FRED

JANKE (ABOVE); BOB

CHAPPUIS (BELOW)

CHALMERS "BUMP" ELLIOTT (ABOVE), PART OF MICHIGAN'S SWIFT 1947 BACKFIELD (BELOW)

season schedule. The Notre Dame Fighting Irish dumped such quality opponents as Nebraska (31–0) and Army (27–7) and destroyed the University of Southern California (USC) Trojans 38–7. Meanwhile, Michigan, led by its dynamic backfield duo of Robert Chappuis and Chalmers (Bump) Elliot, edged a tough Minnesota squad 13–6 and squeaked past Illinois 14–7. Michigan's small margins of victory led many sportswriters to rank the Wolverines second in the national polls behind the Irish.

Michigan responded to the ranking snub by crushing USC 49–0 in the Rose Bowl, demonstrating that it could give the Trojans an even bigger thumping than the Fighting Irish had. Although sportswriters, coaches, and fans nationwide immediately clamored for a match-up between the two powerhouses, Notre Dame had a strict ban on playing in post-season bowl games. The dream showdown never would take place, leaving the true 1947 national champion unclear. Notre Dame claimed the title by virtue of the final Associated Press (AP) poll, while Michigan cited an unofficial AP post-season poll that awarded them the title.

Would the "Mad Magicians" of Michigan's swift backfield have run roughshod over the larger, slower Irish linemen? Or would the huge, dominating line of the Irish have stuffed Michigan's famed offense? Football fans will never know. "It is really a shame that our two teams didn't get to meet in 1947," Notre Dame's

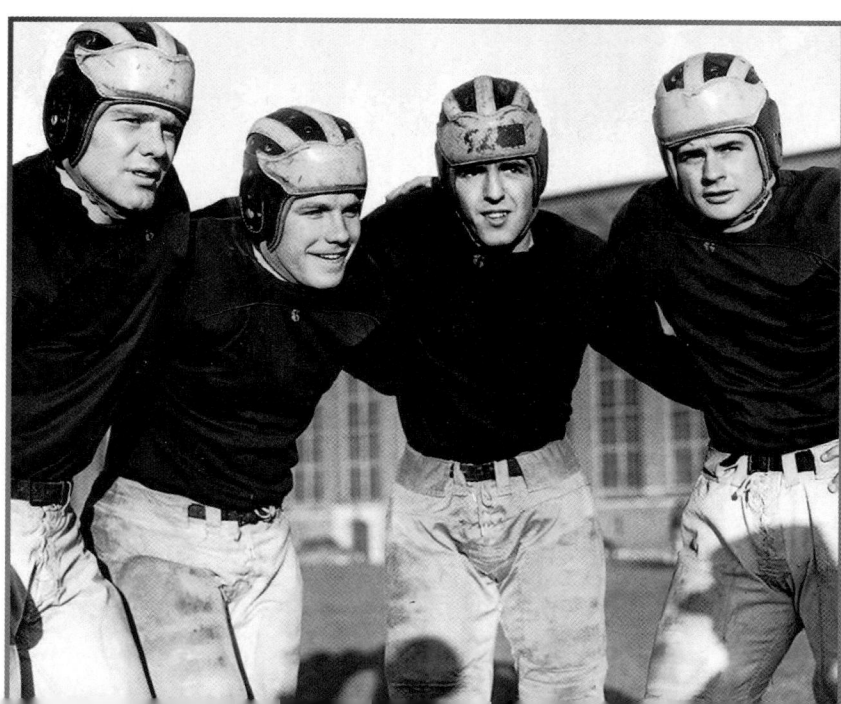

Coach Leahy later said. "Such a game would have given 85,000 football fans a great exhibition of the modern game of football as played by two fine teams."

After Michigan's perfect 1947 season, Fritz Crisler resigned. The architect of the Wolverines' platoon system of inserting different players on offense and defense was finished. One of his star players, a 31-year-old World War II veteran named Alvin Wistert, explained why Crisler gave up coaching. "He told us he did it because the 1947 unit was the greatest team he ever coached," Wistert said. "He said that he would forever set us as the standard, and added that that would be unfair [to later teams]."

## BO'S BOYS

Through the 1950s and '60s, Michigan football went into a tailspin, winning only two Big Ten titles between 1950 and 1968 and suffering an uncharacteristic seven losing seasons. Despite the efforts of such All-Americans as two-way end Ron Kramer, speedy halfback Ron Johnson, and hard-hitting defensive back Rick Volk, the Champions of the West had lost some of their championship luster.

Then, in 1969, Michigan hired a former Ohio State assistant coach by the name of Glenn "Bo" Schembechler. For the next 21 years, Schembechler would drive Michigan to new heights of greatness. During his reign, his teams would go 194–48–5 and produce 39 All-Americans. Schembechler's no-nonsense approach to the game truly fit the Michigan coaching mold of former greats Yost and Crisler.

FULLBACK JACK WEISENBURGER HELPED MICHIGAN TO A 10-0 RECORD IN 1947.

# PLAYER PORTRAIT

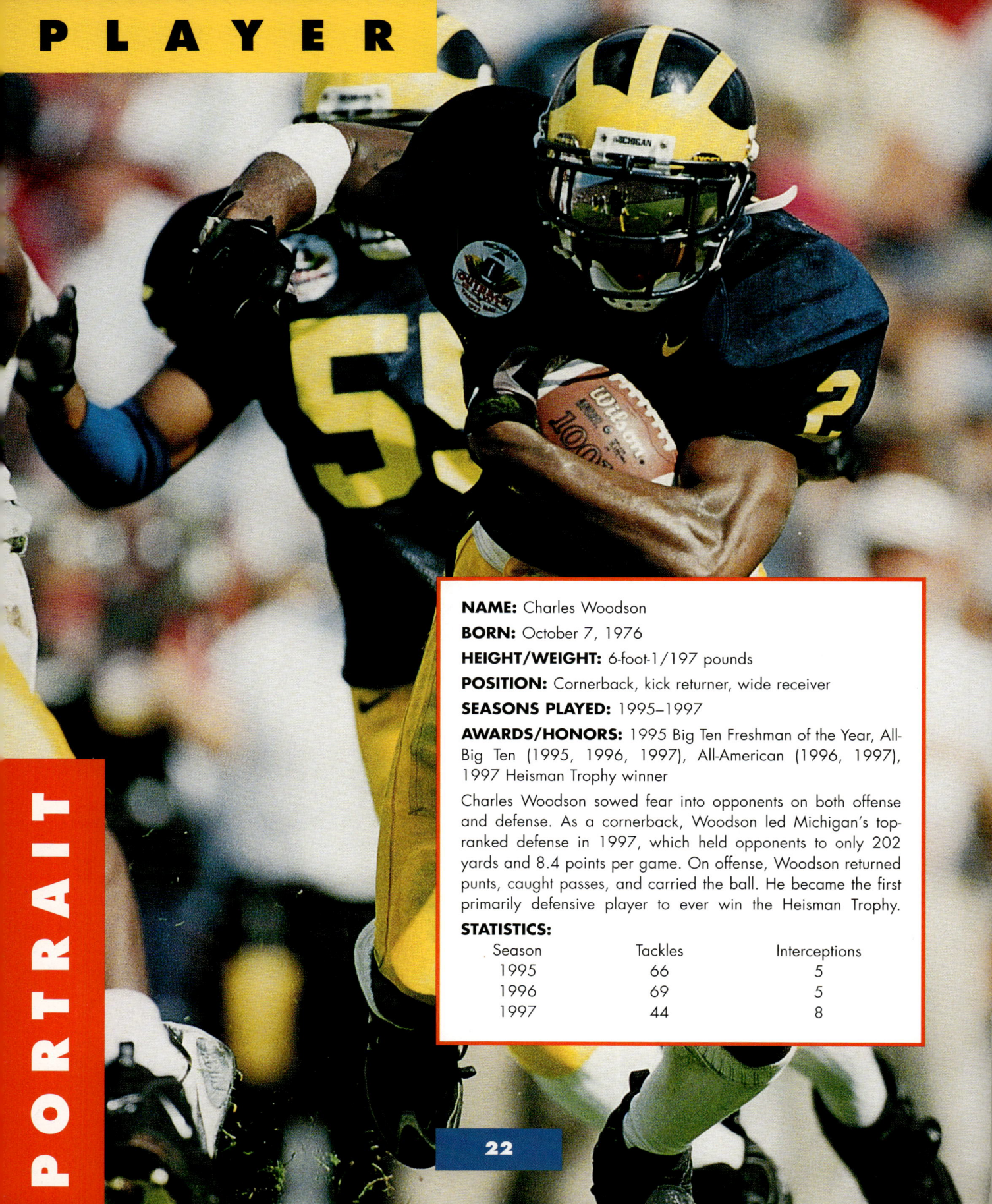

**NAME:** Charles Woodson
**BORN:** October 7, 1976
**HEIGHT/WEIGHT:** 6-foot-1/197 pounds
**POSITION:** Cornerback, kick returner, wide receiver
**SEASONS PLAYED:** 1995–1997
**AWARDS/HONORS:** 1995 Big Ten Freshman of the Year, All-Big Ten (1995, 1996, 1997), All-American (1996, 1997), 1997 Heisman Trophy winner

Charles Woodson sowed fear into opponents on both offense and defense. As a cornerback, Woodson led Michigan's top-ranked defense in 1997, which held opponents to only 202 yards and 8.4 points per game. On offense, Woodson returned punts, caught passes, and carried the ball. He became the first primarily defensive player to ever win the Heisman Trophy.

**STATISTICS:**

| Season | Tackles | Interceptions |
|--------|---------|---------------|
| 1995 | 66 | 5 |
| 1996 | 69 | 5 |
| 1997 | 44 | 8 |

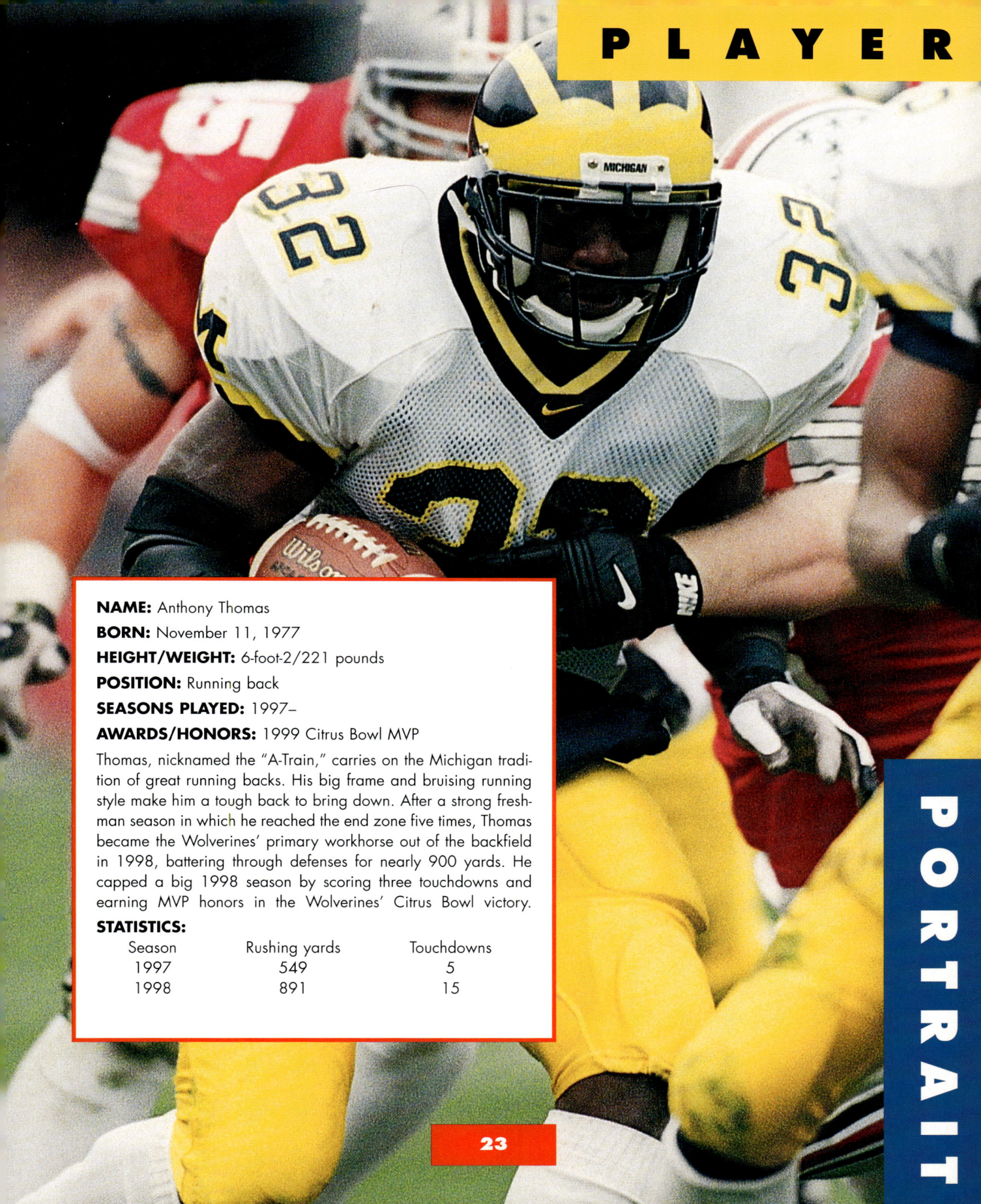

# PLAYER PORTRAIT

**NAME:** Anthony Thomas
**BORN:** November 11, 1977
**HEIGHT/WEIGHT:** 6-foot-2/221 pounds
**POSITION:** Running back
**SEASONS PLAYED:** 1997–
**AWARDS/HONORS:** 1999 Citrus Bowl MVP

Thomas, nicknamed the "A-Train," carries on the Michigan tradition of great running backs. His big frame and bruising running style make him a tough back to bring down. After a strong freshman season in which he reached the end zone five times, Thomas became the Wolverines' primary workhorse out of the backfield in 1998, battering through defenses for nearly 900 yards. He capped a big 1998 season by scoring three touchdowns and earning MVP honors in the Wolverines' Citrus Bowl victory.

**STATISTICS:**

| Season | Rushing yards | Touchdowns |
|--------|---------------|------------|
| 1997 | 549 | 5 |
| 1998 | 891 | 15 |

ANTHONY CARTER WAS ONE

OF COLLEGE FOOTBALL'S

MOST CAPTIVATING STARS.

Critics labeled Coach Schembechler's rush-oriented, "three yards and a cloud of dust" offense as boring. But what some considered boring, others embraced as coldly efficient. His teams' solid, steady, and brutish play was largely responsible for the Big Ten's "black and blue" reputation. What no one could doubt, however, was Michigan's success; Schembechler's teams won or tied for the conference title 13 times in his 21 years.

Still, critics lambasted Schembechler for his disappointing 6–11 record in bowl games. His large, immobile players, detractors said, were no match for the speedsters of west coast teams and squads from the South. Although Schembechler's 2–8 record in

Rose Bowl games was a disappointment to Michigan fans, the Wolverines appeared in 17 bowl games in his 21-year tenure—a remarkable feat.

Schembechler credited his coaching success to the great athletes who played for him at Ann Arbor. One such standout was quarterback Rick Leach, who followed a record-setting collegiate career by playing professional baseball for the Detroit Tigers. Another skilled player who prospered under Schembechler was wide receiver Anthony Carter, a three-time All-American and the most exciting playmaker Wolverines fans had ever seen. The 5-foot-11 and 160-pound receiver earned 1982 Big Ten Most Valuable Player honors and later enjoyed an outstanding career with the Minnesota Vikings. "Having great athletes like A.C. (Anthony Carter) always made me look like a smart coach," said Schembechler.

During Schembechler's tenure at Michigan, the school's bitter rivalry with conference foe Ohio State reached new levels of intensity. Schembechler greatly admired his former mentor at OSU, coaching legend Woody Hayes, and the student's desire to best the teacher burned in Schembechler. Both fiery coaches ran grinding, ball-control running attacks on offense and built rock-ribbed, hard-hitting defenses. Each season until Hayes stepped down in 1978, the Michigan-Ohio State game was more than a football contest—it was a muscle-and-bone chess match between two brilliant football minds. With the stellar play of Wolverines greats such as Leach, Carter, tackle Dan Dierdorf, halfback William Taylor, and defensive back Thom Darden, Schembechler pounded out a 5–4–1 winning record against Hayes.

QUARTERBACK RICK LEACH (ABOVE); COACHING GREAT BO SCHEMBECHLER (BELOW)

25

After a Rose Bowl defeat against USC on January 1, 1990, Bo Schembechler called it quits at the age of 60. He had led his final team to a 10–2 record and a number-eight ranking. Although Schembechler's fine career ended with a loss, his 194 total Wolverines victories assured him a place in Ann Arbor's Hall of Fame.

## CHAMPIONSHIP GLORY

Michigan football after Schembechler continued under the guidance of Gary Moeller, a long-time Michigan assistant and former Illinois head coach. Moeller's teams, sparked by the electrifying performances of Heisman Trophy-winning receiver and kick returner Desmond Howard, brought home four bowl victories during his five years as Michigan's head man. Then, in 1995, after Moeller made inappropriate comments to other customers after drinking too much at a Detroit restaurant, he resigned as coach.

Interim coach Lloyd Carr, also a long-time Michigan assistant, then took over the program and led the Wolverines to two straight 5–3 conference records. Although Carr was finally named the permanent head coach, he knew that his job was in jeopardy unless he could produce more wins. Fortunately, Coach Carr's 1997 squad included two players who would turn things around:

WOLVERINES QUARTERBACKS

TODD COLLINS (ABOVE)

AND TOM BRADY (RIGHT)

cornerback Charles Woodson and quarterback Brian Griese.

Some football experts considered Charles Woodson the best all-around football player since Deion Sanders. Like Sanders, Woodson played defense, returned kicks, and occasionally came in to spark the offense as a receiver. The blazing fast native of Freemont, Ohio, could seemingly beat teams by himself. "The best college player in America," *Sports Illustrated* football reporter Tim Layden wrote in 1997, "has been junior Charles Woodson of Michigan. He is a 6-1, 198-pound cornerback-punt returner-multiple offensive threat who has been at the core of the Wolverines' rise to number one."

While Woodson anchored a rock-solid defense, the steady hand of Brian Griese guided the Wolverines offense through a perfect Big Ten season. Griese, a walk-on quarterback and son of famous Miami Dolphins great Bob Griese, almost gave up football his senior year. He had already been at Michigan for four years, and it appeared that the starting quarterback spot would go to Scott Dreisbach. But with encouragement from his older brother and his father, Griese decided to return for his senior year—a lucky stroke of fate for Wolverines' fans.

Through the entire 1997 season, opposing teams targeted Griese as the weak link in the Wolverines' offense and challenged

COACH CARR (ABOVE) TOOK MICHIGAN TO THE 1997 ROSE BOWL, WHERE GRIESE (BELOW) SHINED.

**PROLIFIC RECEIVER**

**DERRICK ALEXANDER**

**CAUGHT 11 TOUCHDOWN**

**PASSES IN 1992.**

him to throw deep. Opponents thought that if they blitzed Griese hard, they could take Michigan down. Although their plans never slowed the Wolverines, the media continued to doubt Griese's talent right up until Michigan's Rose Bowl showdown against the Washington State Huskies. Reporters heaped praise on Washington State's junior quarterback Ryan Leaf while questioning Griese's ability to handle pressure. The night before the game, Michigan coach Lloyd Carr pulled his senior quarterback and said, "Tomorrow is the day to show everybody that the best quarterback on the field is Brian Griese."

Going into the Rose Bowl, Michigan's running attack had pounded out an average of 182 yards a game during the regular season. To stop the run, Washington State brought eight or nine players up along the defensive line, forcing Griese to throw the ball to gain yardage. Griese did, shredding the Huskies defense for 251 yards and three touchdowns on 18-for-30 passing en route to a 21–16 Wolverines victory. Michigan's undefeated season ended with a Rose Bowl victory, and Griese was named the Rose Bowl MVP, an honor not even his father had received.

To cap the perfect season, Charles Woodson became the third Wolverines player to win the Heisman Trophy. "The spark that Charles gives our team is something that can't be matched," Griese said. "I don't think any other player in the country does that for his team."

Michigan ended the season 11–0 and brought home the school's first national championship since 1948. Thousands of Wolverines football fans agreed with the Rose Bowl MVP when he said, "What we did this year, and what we did today, was restore Michigan to its place in college football."

CHARLES WOODSON WAS THE NATION'S PREMIER PLAYER IN 1997.

RUNNING BACK LEROY HOARD HELPED MICHIGAN CLAIM THE 1989 BIG TEN TITLE.

## PRESERVING THE TRADITION

After soaring to the national championship in 1997, Michigan found the going tougher in 1998. With Woodson and Griese gone to the National Football League, the maize and blue dropped their first two games of the season. But behind the outstanding leadership of quarterback Tom Brady, receiver Tai Streets, and linebacker Sam Sword, the Wolverines roared to eight consecutive victories before losing at Ohio State 31–16. "This is Michigan, and we don't give up here, ever," the fiery Sword said. "There is tradition here built on the shoulders of a lot of guys who came before us. We mean to keep that going."

Michigan finished 7–1 in the Big Ten, good enough for a three-way tie for the conference title with Wisconsin and Ohio State. The resurgent Wolverines capped their season with a 45–31 victory over Arkansas in the Florida Citrus Bowl and finished with a 10–3 record.

With another great season in the books, hopes for future Michigan greatness lie with young stars such as halfback Anthony "A-Train" Thomas. The 6-foot-2 and 221-pound bruiser, nicknamed for his powerful running style, gained 800 yards in 1998, splitting time with speedy Justin Fargas in the backfield. At quarterback, highly recruited prep star Drew Henson from Brighton, Michigan, has the potential to be the next great signal-caller for the Wolverines. On defense, linebackers Ian Gold and Dhani Jones both have the tremendous speed and ferocious hitting instincts to anchor a fierce Wolverines defense.

"We have a solid core of young men who have great ability combined with a great desire to win," said Coach Carr. "Michigan football is in good hands." With a nucleus of potential All-Americans already in place and more talent pouring in each year, it's a good bet that it won't be 50 years before Michigan Stadium is home to a national champion once more.